Saving Castle Clover

by Evelyn Hedges
illustrated by Dani Jones

Harcourt
SCHOOL PUBLISHERS

Printed in China

ISBN 10: 0-15-351508-2
ISBN 13: 978-0-15-351508-8

Ordering Options
ISBN 10: 0-15-351213-X (Grade 3 Advanced Collection)
ISBN 13: 978-0-15-351213-1 (Grade 3 Advanced Collection)
ISBN 10: 0-15-358098-4 (package of 5)
ISBN 13: 978-0-15-358098-7 (package of 5)

2 3 4 5 6 7 8 9 10 985 12 11 10 09 08 07

Castle Clover, in its day, was the finest of the many castles built by the great King Equinor. King Equinor had built a ring of castles around the edges of his empire. In the hard days of the past, the castles were used to help defend the kingdom from enemies. The castles were well prepared with stout walls and high towers, good wells for water, and many supply rooms. The castles were beautiful, too. The most beautiful castle of all was Castle Clover.

Workers had used great white stones to build Castle Clover. The stones dazzled in the sunshine. They glowed in the moonlight, too. Castle Clover could be seen for miles.

As a young stallion, King Equinor had loved the feel of the wind in his mane when he charged down hills at full speed. His fondness for the wind led him to put a flag on every tower of the castle. The flags fluttered gracefully in the wind.

Alas, King Equinor was no longer young. His kingdom had been calm for many years. While peace was good for the decent folk of the kingdom, Equinor paid no attention to them. His subjects never saw him.

"I have nothing to do," he thought. Instead of visiting his kingdom, he stayed in a castle at the edge of the kingdom, eating too many oats, and dreaming of days long past.

Equinor was mistaken when he said he had nothing to do, of course. His subjects wanted to see him. They wanted him to know them. They wanted him to care about them. As years went by, whole families grew up with only stories of their king. To inherit the glory of the tales from others was not the same as to actually see the horse who had earned that glory.

The castles began to fall apart. The worst was Castle Clover. The once-gleaming walls turned gray and dingy. Rocks began to crumble. Water in the wells grew muddy. The inner rooms began to rot. The flags became tattered rags.

The townsfolk at the castle did what they could. They cleaned as far as they could reach. They mended the faded flags. They tried to invent ways to replace stones. What they needed was the help and wealth that only their king could give.

"We must inform the king of this problem," said an elder. Letter after letter was sent to Equinor. They invited him for visits. They asked for advice. They begged for aid. None of the letters was answered.

The situation grew desperate. A falling block nearly struck a young goat. A new emotion took hold. Harsh words were said about the once-beloved king.

The castle folk held a meeting. Speaker after speaker presented ideas. None seemed to offer much hope. "I predict our home will soon be a ruin," said another elder. "We may as well leave."

It was Bitty Hedgehog who asked, "Why was the castle built, anyway?"

"To prevent others from harming us," answered the elder.

"What if someone *were* coming?" asked Bitty.

"That's *it*!" exclaimed Gretel Goose excitedly.

"What is it?" the others asked.

"Let's send an emergency message. We'll tell the king that someone is coming to harm us!"

"We cannot lie to the king," said Hal Horse.

"Well," said Gretel, "maybe we could tell him an important visitor is coming."

"I have just such a visitor in mind," said Orton Owl, smiling.

Orton carefully wrote the message. The pigeons flew it to the palace. They rested tiredly on the walls, and then they dived at the First Minister. "You must take this to the king," they said. "Tempus is coming!"

The First Minister did take the message to King Equinor. "Who is this Tempus?" asked the king.

"I know not, Your Highness. Orton, the wisest owl of Castle Clover, says here that the visit cannot be prevented."

"I remember Orton," said the king. "He was always a bright one."

A change came over King Equinor. "Prepare," he said to all the ministers. "We will go to Castle Clover. We will meet this great visitor."

For the first time in years, King Equinor and his court left home. In full glory, the king and his followers moved along the road. "This feels good," the king said.

When the king arrived at Castle Clover, he could not believe how awful it looked. "It used to be so beautiful," he said. Then he summoned Orton. "Has Tempus arrived yet?"

"It is my understanding," said Orton, "that Tempus could be here any minute."

"We must get to work then," said Equinor. "Tempus shall not find the castle in such a ridiculous and disgraceful condition."

With his old energy, King Equinor restored the castle. He directed all the work. His army repaired the walls. Other troops brought lumber and fixed buildings. They dug the wells deeper to reach clear water. Each day Equinor asked, "Is there news of the arrival of Tempus?"

"Tempus is always on the move," Orton said. "He will be here at any moment."

At last, Castle Clover took on its former beauty. The king looked around. "We are ready," he said.

Orton spoke to King Equinor. "Your Highness," he said. "I have something to tell you."

"About Tempus, Owl?" asked King Equinor. "I've felt you knew more than you were saying."

"Yes, " said Orton. "Tempus is already here."

"Here! Where? Show me this visitor."

Orton swallowed and said, "*Tempus* means 'Time,' my King. It was *Time* that took you away. It was *Time* that harmed the castle walls. Now *Time* has brought you back. In saving Castle Clover, you have decided to use your *Time* well and not to waste it."

Equinor stared at Orton. "*Tempus* is *Time*," he said slowly. Then he looked around at the restored castle. He looked at the lovely flags, flying as the wind had once flown in his mane. "I realize now that you are right. I have not always used my time well." Then he laughed. "A festival!" he proclaimed. "Let us have a festival in honor of Tempus!"

A few days later, the folk of Castle Clover feasted with King Equinor. The king knew that he could not recover the time that he had wasted, but he could do good and useful things with the time he had left.

Think Critically

1. Who is telling this tale?

2. Why isn't King Equinor angry at Orton for the trick that has been played?

3. Why does King Equinor decide to go out after so many years and visit Castle Clover?

4. What does King Equinor think Tempus is? What is it really?

5. What details in this story interested you? Why?

Social Studies

Design a Flag In olden days, nobles decorated flags with artwork that showed facts about their kingdom. Design and draw a flag that shows some facts about your hometown.

 School-Home Connection This story is about how time passes. Talk to friends and family members about how people change over time. Ask them to tell you a story about when you were younger and how you have changed.